LITTLE CAPTAIN

CLAUDIO MUÑOZ

RED FOX

A Red Fox Book

Published by Random House Children's Books
20 Vauxhall Bridge Road, London SW1V 2SA

A division of The Random House Group Ltd
London Melbourne Sydney Auckland
Johannesburg and agencies throughout the world

Copyright © Claudio Munoz 1995

3 5 7 9 10 8 6 4 2

First published in Great Britain by The Bodley Head Children's Books 1995
Red Fox edition 1997
This edition 2000

Printed in Singapore by Tien Wah Press (PTE) Ltd

THE RANDOM HOUSE GROUP Ltd Reg. No. 954009
www.randomhouse.co.uk

His dog bounced happily
in front and chased a
seagull.

The seagull stopped and
where she stopped the
dog began to dig.

At the bottom of the
hole, damp and
scratched, Lucien
found Little Captain.

In bed that night Lucien held Little Captain tight, right close
to his ear. 'Now you can tell me what really happened,' he
whispered. And Lucien closed his eyes and listened
to the story . . .

Aren't boats wonderful things?
    Lucien could watch them for ever sailing in and out of the
harbour.

And Grandad knew lots of stories about sailing. He had once been a sailor himself.

One day at the market Lucien found an old model boat. Many years ago it had belonged to another child, who had thrown it away once it became old and shabby.

They took it home and repaired it. How different it looked with
its new colours and that very odd set of sails! (Those were the
only spare bits of material Grandma could find.)

Lucien was delighted and, for no particular reason, decided to
call it The Star.

But what was Grandad doing?
Wait, Lucien, don't look yet!

That evening Grandad gave
Lucien a little wooden figure. It
was a handsome little captain
with a black beard, in a blue
uniform and white cap.

After Grandma and Grandad kissed him goodnight, Lucien looked closely at the little figure. It seemed to look back at him.

And that night he held the captain tight as he snuggled down to sleep.

The next day, Lucien had hardly
finished his breakfast before he
ran down to the river with the
boat and its captain.
The Star sailed beautifully and
Little Captain stood high on the
deck. A noisy seagull appeared
above them.

Was it saying something to Little Captain? I don't know, but The Star turned and began to sail away, following the seagull. Lucien ran along the bank and shouted, 'Stop!' and 'Come back!' until the boat, captain and seagull turned a bend and he could see them no more.

Down the river sailed The Star and Little Captain,
the seagull always in front.

Under willow trees and bridges, past fields and
quiet villages; then the river widened and they
streamed by boatyards and warehouses, big
buildings and massive ships . . .

. . . until they reached the open sea.

Little Captain followed the seagull
towards ominous dark clouds.
Astonished sailors watched
them brave the storm.

Then in the distance a lonely figure
waved and shouted, adrift on her broken boat.

Oh, the disappointment when she saw it was only a toy!

But she never saw Little Captain make a dash for the cabin . . .

. . . or disappear inside the broken radio. She never knew
that he repaired it so that she could now call for help.

But worst of all she never
knew that Little Captain
was trapped and couldn't
get out at all.

Then the rescue helicopter roared overhead
and the lonely sailor was lifted up to safety.
Down below, her boat smashed against the
cliffs. Help had come just in time.

  The sailor held on tightly to The Star. 'My
lucky star,' she sighed.

Look at poor Lucien.

All day he searched the river bank in vain. Little Captain and The Star seemed to have vanished.

Grandma and Grandad tried their best to cheer him up, but it wasn't easy: they were quite sad themselves.

The news that evening showed pictures of a sea rescue. The woman interviewed was holding The Star!

'Lucien, she's got it!' Grandad rushed to the phone.

Was Little Captain there? It was hard to tell.

Some days later the sailor called in. She gave The Star back to
Lucien, saying, 'I'm sorry the little captain is lost. I feel sure he
helped me, though I'll never know how.'

Lucien tried hard not to cry, but managed to say, 'Thank you.'
Was there any hope of ever seeing Little Captain again? He
was going to miss him.

The holidays were over. One lovely autumn day after school,
Lucien went to play on the beach.